MOUNTAIN MAN'S VIRGIN

MEN OF MAPLE MOUNTAIN BOOK THREE

SADIE KING

Her ambition got her up the mountain. But when this burly mountain man spies her curves, he won't let her go...

I'm not an outdoors person, I'm scared of the wild.

So how did I end up halfway up a mountain in a flimsy tent? I lied, that's how. A big, massive stonking lie to get my first break.

But I didn't count on Chase. The rugged mountain guide who's making me sweat more than I should.

A night in the wild turns from my biggest fear into my most pleasurable adventure.

But what happens when the trail ends? Can I ever go back to my old life, or has the mountain claimed me for good?

Mountain Man's Virgin is a short and steamy, forced-proximity, city girl/mountain man romance featuring an OTT obsessed hero and the curvy woman he claims as his own. A safe read with no cliffhangers and a happily ever after guaranteed.

BROOKLYN

My fingers tap along to the music, connected through my phone and blaring through the car speakers.

Bringing my takeout coffee cup to my lips, I take a sip just as my ringtone blasts through the speakers, making me jump and causing hot coffee to splash over my legs.

"Shoot."

Keeping one eye on the road, I set the coffee down in the cup holder. Patting at the stain spreading across my crotch, I answer on handsfree.

"Hey babe, you there yet?" Lilia's bubbly voice comes at me through the car speakers.

"The last sign of civilization was Maple Springs about twenty minutes ago and there's a big ass mountain in front of me, so yeah, I guess I'm almost there."

"I'm so excited for you," she squeals, making me wince and turn the volume down a notch.

"Thanks babe."

Lilia's my best friend, ever since we met at college and then started interning together at Durant Magazine Group. We both want to be journalists one day and she's as excited as I am to get my first proper assignment.

"Thought I should warn you; Kelvin was asking some tricky questions."

Kelvin's the editor of Mountain Travel magazine, one of the magazines that Durant owns, and the guy I blatantly lied to get this assignment.

"What was he asking?"

"He asked me about our hike to Mt. Hood."

My body tenses. I've never been to Mt. Hood. I've never been to any mountain in my life. But when the journalist who was booked to write the piece on the Maple Mountain trails broke his leg, I pleaded to be given the assignment.

I told Kelvin I was outdoorsy and loved hiking, which might have been a big lie. And I might have accidentally told him that me and Lilia went hiking together.

Finally, he gave in and let me go. After all, it was already paid for and set up. We've got a mountain guide waiting for us in Maple Falls.

"What did you say?" I sip my coffee nervously,

wondering if Lilia is about to tell me I have to turn around and come home.

"I told him it was awesome."

My body relaxes. This is why Lilia's my best friend.

"Thank you. I'm sorry I mentioned you, it just accidentally slipped out."

"Don't worry about it, babe. I know you're going to be awesome out there. You got this."

Her words make me smile and set me a little at ease. I wish I could have as much confidence in myself as Lilia does in me.

"Thanks hon. How's thing's back in the office?"

Lilia starts to reply but the phone goes dead. With my eyes on the road, I hit call back but it goes straight to answerphone. I glance at my phone and there's no bars, no signal.

"Great." I'm really in the sticks now.

A tremor of doubt runs through me. I wonder, not for the first time, if I should turn around and head back to Seattle. I've never been hiking in my life; my body isn't built for it. I'm short and round and I prefer binge reading in my sweatpants than galivanting around in nature.

But after three months making coffee and checking print runs, I was desperate to get some real experience. When I saw an opportunity, I took it. I mean how difficult can a two-day hike be.

All I've got to do is walk up a mountain with a

trained guide, make some notes, and write a nice piece about the trail.

I've been studying the magazine, and I know the type of thing I need to write. Describe the scenery, mention the wildlife, talk about the peacefulness, recharging from the city, yada yada yada. Easy.

The only thing I'm concerned about is the night that we have to camp on the mountain.

Spending a night in a tent in the middle of nowhere makes me shudder. But I've pushed that out of my mind, trying not to think about it. If it gets me my big journalist break, then one sleepless night will be worth it.

The sat nav tells me to turn left for Maple Falls. It's a gravel road with a wooden signpost that looks like it hasn't changed since the 19th century.

"It's just two days."

I prepare myself. Two days in the ass end of nowhere. Do the hike, get the story, and get out. How hard can it be?

The first houses of Maple Falls come in to view. They're more like cabins than houses. Set off the street, up steep driveways, peeping out from between leafy trees. It's quaint, nicer than I expected.

The Main Street, if you can call it that, consists of a line of boutique shops. I slow down, taking in the scattered buildings that line the street. There's a couple of hiking shops, fishing supplies stores, a post office, a convenience store, and a cute looking café.

At the end of the street is a bar, Bear's Brewery. It's got prime position overlooking the mountain.

The tourist office sits across the road, and I pull into a parking space wedging my Mazda hatchback between two enormous pick-up trucks. Both mud splattered, not like the shiny ones on the streets of Seattle.

My coffee is still warm, and I clutch it in one hand, phone in the other, as I enter the tourist office. A kind looking middle-aged lady in thick glasses looks up at the sound of the door.

"Welcome to Maple Falls. How can I help?"

"I'm here to meet someone." I set the coffee down and scroll through my inbox looking for the email with the name of the person I'm supposed to meet. Thankfully there's one bar of signal here.

There's the sound of the door opening and shutting behind me which brings a cool breeze and makes my hairs stand on end.

I find the email. "Chase Amery. I'm doing a walk with him."

"A hike, not a walk." The deep voice comes from behind, making me jump and almost spill my coffee again. I spin around and my heart skitters in my chest.

Standing behind me is without a doubt the hottest man I've ever laid eyes on. He's tall, at least six feet, with shaggy sandy colored hair and pale blue eyes that are staring at me with an intensity that makes me blush.

"Ah-are- you Chase?" I only just mange to get the words out of my mouth because it's gone bone dry.

His pale eyes sweep up my body and land on my breasts. I'm used to men looking at my breasts; they're bigger than average due to my weight being bigger than average. Usually, I hate it, but for once I don't mind him looking.

In fact, I want him to keep that gaze on me, I want him to look at my whole body that way, with a hungry look.

"You don't look like a Scott." His eyes dance and a smile plays at the corner of his lips.

"I'm um…" So distracted by him I can't think straight. Pulling myself together and remembering why I'm here, I step forward with my hand outstretched. "I'm Brooklyn. Scott broke his leg so they sent me."

"Chase." He takes my hand and presses it against his.

His palm is rough with calluses, and a flash of heat races up my arm, wondering what that hand would feel like running over my body.

I drop my hand quickly and drop my head to look at my phone, trying to hide the blush that's climbing up my neck.

This assignment just got a whole lot more interesting.

2

CHASE

The woman in front of me is like a vision from heaven. Wide grabbable hips, long thick blonde hair. Bent over her phone, she's giving me a good view of the v shape of her cleavage, peeping out between the top of her t-shirt.

Perfect round tits and the sweetest pouty lips I ever saw. Damn, she's a fine-looking woman.

She's peering at her phone as if that's going to save her from my lascivious thoughts.

"Um, we're doing a two-day hike..."

"Three days."

She looks up suddenly; her honey-colored eyes show her confusion.

"The email I got from Scott says two days."

I'm sure it does. Two days up the mountain with someone called Scott would have been enough. But they've sent the curvy Brooklyn with the amazing tits. I'm making it three days.

"Three days, two nights to see the lakes. They're the jewel of the mountain, I'm sure you want to write about them."

She looks hesitant. "Two nights camping?"

My eyes run over her jeans, light t-shirt, and trainers. She doesn't look like someone who's prepared for the mountain.

"You've got hiking boots, right?"

"Yes." She gives me a huge grin. I don't understand why she's so happy she's got hiking boots, but fuck me, it lights up her eyes making them dance like honey trickling off a spoon.

I have a sudden vision of licking honey off her curvy body.

The blood runs to my dick and I have to turn away or she'll see my hard on and run all the way back down the mountain.

"Good." I head for the door. Not wanting to leave but needing to get away from her before I do something stupid. "You staying at The Crown?"

It's the only hotel in town and she nods.

"I'll pick you up at 5.30 tomorrow."

Her mouth almost hits the floor. "In the morning?"

I give her one of my most charming smiles. "Gotta start early if we want to get to the lakes."

I leave her gapping after me. There is no way that

woman has ever been hiking in her life. I'm not sure what her angle is, but I'm determined to find out.

It's still dark the next morning when I pull up at The Crown. It's dead on 5.30 and I expect to be waiting for a while, but Brooklyn surprises me. She comes out of the hotel looking adorable in khakis so new they've still got the crease down the front and a much too big backpack.

"Morning," I say cheerfully.

She shoots me a look that lets me know she may be up but she's not happy about it. I hold out a hot thermos.

"Coffee?"

Her face lights up and the smile goes straight to my heart. I love that it doesn't take much to change her mood. I'm an easy-going guy myself and I hate grumpy people. Apart from my brother, he's the only grumpy person I can stand.

She's struggling under her backpack, and I slip it off her shoulders and undo the zip.

"Hey," she protests.

"I need to check your pack, make sure you've got the right things, and not too much."

"Why wouldn't I have the right things?" She grabs the bag off me defensively and I wonder what she's hiding.

"Relax, I do this with all my clients. The mountain

can be an unforgiving place. The weather can change, an accident could happen, we could meet a bear and have to divert our path, I need to make sure we're prepared for all eventualities."

She's gone white. "There are bears on the mountain?"

I'm so used to living with bears that I forget how freaked out some people get, although I would have thought a journalist working for a mountain hiking magazine wouldn't be in that category.

"Only black bears and they mostly stick to the higher ground. We're unlikely to see one."

"Okay." Her voice seems strained, and I change the subject.

I go through her bag, chucking out two sets of sweaters, a pair of jeans, and a roll up pillow.

"Use your jacket as your pillow, it saves on space."

Her gear is a mixture of well-worn and brand-new, and I wonder again what her angle is. In the top of her backpack, she's got a phone, and I take it out and put it in the 'do not need' pile.

"Whoa, that's coming with us." She picks it up. "I don't go anywhere without my phone."

She sticks her chin out defiantly, a real city girl, not wanting to be parted from her tech.

"Suit yourself, but I'm not taking mine."

"But what if something happens to us?"

"What's gonna happen?"

"Like, any of those things you just mentioned. Change in weather, a bear…"

She's working herself up, and she looks adorable. I resist the urge to run my hands over her, to touch her in any way.

"Relax, I always tell the ranger where we're going, so if we don't come back, they'll know exactly where to find us."

She doesn't look impressed. "That sounds slow."

"Yeah, it is. Life moves at a slower pace on the mountain, give it a try, you might like it." She looks down at her phone. "There's no signal once we leave town anyway."

She slips the phone in her back pocket. "I might want to take pictures," she says defiantly.

I shrug. City folk are always tied to their tech. I'm not going to fight her on it.

Once I've done the inventory, her bag's lighter by about half. Finally, we're ready to go and I drive the few miles to the ranger's hut and where the trail begins. I leave a note for Kit letting him know where we're going and when we'll be back. Then, shouldering our packs, we set off up the mountain.

3

BROOKLYN

There's a burning sensation in my thighs, and my back aches from carrying the backpack. Thank goodness Chase got rid of half my stuff out of it before we set off.

My ankles chafe every time I take a step, and I'm sure I'm going to find a fat blister when I eventually peel off my sock. It was lucky I found a pair of hiking boots in my size at the charity shop, but there was no time to wear them in.

It was hours ago that we set off in the faint glow of daybreak. The pale predawn light was just enough to show us a path to the first ridge where we stopped for breakfast.

The sky was streaked with pink as we finished the coffee and ate the bagels that Chase had brought. One good thing about hiking, you must eat a lot of carbs because you need the energy to burn.

We broke for lunch in a forest clearing surrounded by a sea of wildflowers. I've never seen such a vibrant purple in nature before.

But lunch seems like a long time ago as we slog up the winding path. My body aches in places I never knew existed, and this is only day one.

Chase is ahead of me, and I watch his confident figure as he takes long strides, skirting easily around the dips and rock piles of the path. Like a large, good looking mountain goat. If a mountain goat can be good looking.

Every so often he pauses to let me catch up with him. And when he does, I try to get my heaving breath under control and smile like I'm enjoying myself. Although somewhere between the sunrise and lunch, the smile became genuine and I realized I am enjoying myself.

And a lot of that is down to Chase. We've been singing as we walk. Belting out eighties' ballads and nineties hip hop.

He makes me laugh almost as much as Lilia does. Except when I laugh with Chase, I get a funny feeling in my tummy, like I want to throw my arms around him and squeeze him tight. Which is crazy because I only just met him.

· · ·

The path widens and we come to a clearing in the scrub with a rock ledge behind us. Chase sits on a boulder, and I shrug off my pack to join him.

"We'll stay here for the night."

We're in a dip and the mountain is hidden by the stack of boulders. I imagined breaking camp somewhere a little more scenic.

"Why here?"

Chase gives me a mysterious smile. "You'll see."

He gets to work gathering wood for a fire and instructs me to get the tents pitched.

Pulling the yellow canvas out of my pack, I pretend to know what I'm doing. I've never pitched a tent in my life but I can't let Chase know that.

There are some sticks that seem to join to make a long pole. I get that bit figured out but am struggling to find the holes to put them in.

I look up to find Chase watching me.

"Different to the tent I have at home," I mumble.

"Here." He takes the end off me and shoves it through an opening in the canvas, he feeds it through till it pokes out the other end. "Now put it in that metal ring at the bottom."

He doesn't ask me why I don't know how to put up a tent, but it's obvious he's on to me. Not that it matters now. We're halfway up the mountain, there's no going back.

By the time the tents are up, the sun is low in the sky throwing the surroundings into a golden light.

"I want to show you something."

Chase puts this hand out to me, and I take it, feeling it fit snugly into his. He leads me carefully around the rock face to where some boulders stick out making it easy to climb up, like stairs. I follow him up the rock face and we come out onto a flat ledge about ten feet above our camp.

On the other side of the rocks is a ridge that drops away to the valley below.

"This is what I wanted you to see."

The valley is laid out before us, with Maple Falls in the distance and further down the mountain I can make out the winding road that leads down to Maple Springs, the bigger town beyond.

The sun is a burnt orange in the sky as it sets behind the valley.

"It's beautiful."

He grins. "Thought you'd like it."

And I do. We sit without speaking for a long time, watching the sky change from orange to gold to pink.

"Have you always lived on the mountain?" I ask.

"All my life. My mother was a cleaner at the Crown Hotel. Me and my brother grew up roaming around the mountain."

"Does your brother still live here?"

His eyes crinkle and he laughs, something he does often. "Oh yeah. Rowan's a grumpy old recluse."

Chase is so good natured I can't imagine how a sibling of his could be anything different.

"He's ex-military," he tells me. "Prefers to live alone. Hardly ever comes down the mountain."

I try to imagine what it's like, growing up here. I grew up in Seattle. My parents took me to the beach sometimes, but they weren't into the outdoors. I wonder why not, as I watch the sky turn to pink and breath in the fresh mountain air.

"Come on," Chase says eventually. "We better eat dinner before the bears come sniffing around."

My body tenses. I can't tell if he's being serious or not. His chuckle reaches me through the half-light.

"I'm joking, there's no bears."

I laugh uneasily. That's all a city girl like me hears about the wild, that there's bears and things that could hurt you. No one tells you about the sunsets and sunrises and purple flowers and the sounds of birds.

I scramble down the boulder feeling my way in the dim light until I reach the campfire. Taking a seat on an upturned log, a feeling of peace washes over me as I watch the flames.

I get it now, this hiking. It's wonderful being out in nature, out in the wilderness. It's only been one day, but I think I'm a convert.

A few hours later I'm woken in the night by a rustling in my tent. My heart thunders in my ears as I strain to hear what woke me.

There it is again, a rustling noise, like something's trying to get into my tent. Like a bear's trying to get in.

I sit up, my heart hammering.

"Chase!" I call out, fumbling in the darkness for the torch. "Chase, there's a something out here."

There's the sounds of a zip undoing and a light flicks on.

"Chase!" I call again, panic rising in my chest.

The rustling intensifies as the zip to my tent comes undone. Chase appears in the door of my tent, his hair ruffled and his eyes blurry from sleep.

"What happened?"

"I heard something." My heart's racing. "I think it was a bear." It feels stupid to say it, but he just nods.

"I'll go take a look."

Before I can protest, he ducks out of the tent and I'm left alone in the dark.

I see his light flicking around outside and hear his footsteps as he circles our camp. My heart's in my throat as I wait for him to come back. Eventually his face appears in the tent entrance again.

"No sign of anything out here."

I'm starting to feel slightly stupid, but no less afraid. "I heard something."

He nods sympathetically. "Might have been the wind, or a twig falling on the tent."

"It wasn't a twig, it was something big, some kind of animal." Although now I'm not so sure. What I am sure about is I'm not getting any more sleep tonight.

He starts to retreat. "I'm going back to bed…"

"Don't leave me."

It comes out as a plea, and I know I'm being ridicules but we're on the side of a mountain with nothing but a thin bit of canvas between me and the big scary outdoors.

"Sleep in here, with me."

His body stiffens, and I wonder if that's against some kind of trail guide protocol. Don't sleep in the same tents as your clients. But stuff that, I'm scared and I want Chase next to me.

"I feel safe with you," I plead. "Bring your sleeping bag in here, otherwise I won't be able to sleep."

He stares at me for a long time then nods. "Fine. But it's okay. There's nothing to be scared of."

He drags his sleeping bag in and settles down next to me.

It's a small tent, made for one, and with Chase in here, our bodies are pushed up together. Even through the thick layer of sleeping bag, I feel the heat radiating off him. I clench my thighs together. Now that the fear has gone, it's been replaced by a longing in my core. A longing for Chase.

He turns on his side and faces away and a wave of disappointment rushes over me.

I wonder what it would be like to lie next to him, as man and woman, with his arm draped over me.

"I remember my first time sleeping on the mountain," says Chase. "I was with my brother and my dad, when he was still around. We camped out in a big tent, not too far from town. I didn't sleep a wink. Every time the wind blew and the tent rattled, I was sure it was some animal coming to get us."

He rolls over onto his back. "How about you, Brooklyn? When was the first time you slept out in a tent?"

I bite my lower lip, thinking up some lie to tell him, running through plausible scenarios in my head. But there's something about Chase; I don't want to lie to him. I decide on the truth.

"Um, tonight." He doesn't say anything. "Tonight is the first night I've slept in a tent."

"I thought so." Even in the dark I know he's smiling. And I feel relief. He knows my secret and he's not cross.

"Goodnight, Brooklyn."

"Goodnight, Chase."

With him lying next to me, it doesn't take long to drift off to sleep.

4

CHASE

It's the following day as we trudge up the final stretch of the path that leads to the crater lakes. Brooklyn might have slept soundly last night, but I tossed and turned next to her.

Being so close to her was torture. My body was hot all night imagining her touch. I had to restrain myself from reaching out to her in the night.

I settled for watching her sleep instead. Watching the gentle rise and fall of her chest with her lips slightly parted. Laid out like a sweet innocent flower before me. A flower that I want to ravage, tear apart. Satisfy this crazy lust that's been burning through my body ever since I saw her.

But it's more than that. Hanging out with Brooklyn on the mountain has been the most fun I've had in ages. She may be a bad liar, but she's quick to laugh and easy to talk to. I feel like we've known each other a lot longer than just over twenty-four hours.

She's panting hard as we come to the top of the ridge. I take her hand, watching her expression as she looks up at the view

She gasps, which make me smile. I love showing her all the secrets of the mountain and the best one yet has got to be the emerald lakes. Left over from an ancient volcanic eruption, the lakes are carved into the crater, with the peak of the mountain behind them.

The volcanoes are long since extinct, but the crater lakes remain, along with a series of small pools, perfect for swimming.

I shrug off my backpack and peel off my t-shirt.

"What are you doing?" She looks alarmed.

"Going for a swim."

Her eyes run over the tattoos on my chest. I can't say it's a bad feeling, having her eyes on me.

"I didn't bring a swimsuit," she protests.

"Neither did I."

I strip off to my briefs and dive into the cool water. The cold hits me like a brick to the head. The water's straight from the mountain and icy cold, but I'm not going to tell her that.

"Come on in."

Hesitantly, she slides off her pack and her shoes. I turn around and swim to the edge of the pool to give her some privacy. I'm dying to see her body, but I'll get there soon enough. I hear a splash behind me, and then she's gasping and spluttering.

"It's freezing!"

I laugh as she flails about with her arms.

"Keep swimming, you'll get used to it."

She calms her movements and joins me at the edge of the pool giving me a dirty look. "You could have told me it was this cold."

"And miss the fun? Why would I do that?"

She splashes me with water but she's laughing.

"You want a water fight?" I splash her back and we're both laughing and splashing each other. She squeals, her giggle echoing around the rocks. The sun glints on her laughing face making her eyes sparkle. Not able to restrain myself any longer, I grab her around the waist.

She gasps, her mouth popping open in surprise. Those full lips making my dick ache

"Come here."

Pulling her toward me, her soft skin feels smooth under my touch. Then my lips are on hers, pressing against her. She hesitates for a moment, then she's kissing me back. Her lips soft and pliant, her tongue exploring my mouth.

My hands run down her body and over her ass, pulling her toward me. Wanting to make her mine.

The splashing of a moment ago has gone and were both still, treading water as we explore each other's mouths.

She shivers in my arms and I pull away.

"You're cold."

She nods. "It is, like, zero degrees in here."

"Come on. I'll get a fire going."

Leaning on rock ledge, I pull myself out of the water and then help her out. Through her soaking bra, her nipples are dark, pebbling against the cold.

"Lie down in the sun."

She lies on the rock ledge to dry off. The wet fabric clings to her body showing off her mound and the dark patch of hair underneath.

A zing of energy floods my veins and my cock goes rock hard. I've never wanted a woman as much as I want Brooklyn. And now I'm sure she feels the same. My body aches in anticipation.

But the light's starting to fade and the heat of the day with it. I need to get the fire going and get her warm.

Then I can make her mine.

5

BROOKLYN

It's a few hours later and the heat from the fire sends a warm glow up my legs and through my body.

But it's not just the fire that's making me hot. I run my hands over my lips, feeling the impression of Chase.

When I look up, he's staring at me across the flames. The fire inside me intensifies and my skin prickles with heat.

"Brooklyn." He stands up. His voice is raspy and causes the hairs on my neck to stand on end.

It's a few hours since we had the kiss, and my body hasn't stilled since. We've gone about the business of setting up camp, getting the fire going, and eating a basic meal.

Chase takes his job as a guide seriously, and now

he's got the practicalities out the way, his attention turns to me.

And I love it.

He comes around to my side of the fire and takes me by the hand. I tremble at his touch, my whole core burning for him.

"I want to show you something."

He spreads his sleeping bag on the ground next to the campfire.

"Lie down," he says, pulling me onto the sleeping bag.

My lips ready for his kiss, but instead, he lies next to me on his back.

"Look up."

I do as he says and my breath catches in my throat. Above me the sky is ablaze with stars, shimmering like diamonds against the dark sky.

The Milky Way is spread out above us and untold galaxies beyond stretching away to infinity. I've never seen so many stars and never seen them shining so bright.

"It's beautiful," I whisper.

He takes my hand, and we lie for a long time watching the celestial bodies shimmer above us. Eventually he sits up on his elbows and leans toward me. His finger traces the skin of my bare arm making me shiver in anticipation.

"Brooklyn."

Every time he says my name, my pussy clenches, shooting dampness to my panties.

He says it again, this time nuzzling into my neck, his hot breath doing crazy things to my skin.

"I want to make you mine."

His hand slides over my belly and down to the place between my legs. He cups me in his hand. It feels possessive, which should feel wrong, but freakin' heck. It's feels good, so good.

"Chase…"

It comes out as a whine, a whimper. This tension that's been building in my body all day, I want him to release it, but I don't know how to ask.

He seems to sense what I need because his hand slips into the top of my pants and slides into my underwear. His eyes are hooded and dark barely visible against the night sky.

"Lie back, Brooklyn, and watch the stars."

As he says it, he palms my pussy entrance causing the heat inside me to intensify. I gasp as he finds my clit, rubbing his thumb against my most sensitive spot.

My body arches and I sit up on my elbows.

"I've got to tell you something." His hand freezes. "I've not done this before."

"You're a virgin?"

"Yes," I whisper.

His thumb brushes against my clit and I gasp.

"I'll take care of you, baby." He moves so gently, so

softly, strumming my hard nub and waking all the nerves endings in my body.

"Lie back and enjoy it."

I do as he says and this time look upwards to the canopy of stars above.

He slides a finger inside me and groans as my pussy tightens around him. With the stars above and him rubbing my core, I feel the whole of the universe pinpointed to my center as he brings me closer and closer to a single point.

My eyes roll back in my head and the stars blur above me. My body writhes and I push against him, getting nearer and nearer to the center of the universe. Then I explode, energy zipping through my body as I climax and the whole cosmos shifts.

I'm floating outside my body, at one with the universe.

Eventually I float back down to earth and come back to myself, gasping in his arms. His face in the darkness is hard to read. He kisses the side of my mouth as he yanks at my pants. I help him shimmy them off. Wanting more from him, wanting all of him.

He pulls his trousers off and his cock sticks out, thick and hard. My core tugs toward him, the fire inside of me still burning.

"Will it hurt?"

He kneels before me and kisses me gently on the sides of my neck.

"Maybe for a little, but then you'll like it."

His cock brushes my entrance, sending me into throws of ecstasy. Then he pushes inside. There's a burning sensation and I think I can't stand it.

He clutches me close to him and we rock together, my pussy adjusting to this new sensation.

Then the burning turns to pleasure. I'm full up, so full of him and it's indescribably good.

He slides gently back and forth, taking it slowly until I can't stand it anymore.

"Chase."

I grab him round the waist, my hands trailing down to his butt. Digging my nails into him, I pull him toward me. The sensation intensifies and I'm focused on that one singular point again

"Chase, I think I'm going to explode."

"Good," he growls. "Come for me."

He hooks one leg over his shoulder and pumps me hard. It takes me over the edge and I scream out his name. The stars explode above us as my body shatters into a million pieces. Chase slams into me grunting as he releases inside me.

We shudder together joined as one as our bodies writhe.

Afterward, he pulls me close and wraps his arms around me, keeping me warm and safe. We sleep under the stars, two people in this tiny universe clinging together on the top of a mountain.

I've never felt so insignificant, yet so content.

6

CHASE

*D*awn light wakes me the next morning. We spent the night sleeping under the stars, our bodies pressed together for warmth.

Careful not to wake Brooklyn, I stoke the fire and get a pot of water boiling. By the time the coffee's ready, Brooklyn's sitting up, rubbing sleep out of her eyes.

"Morning."

I hand her a mug of coffee and sit next to her, my arm going around her shoulders.

She leans against me as we watch the sky turn from dark to day.

"I don't ever want to leave," she says wistfully.

"Then don't."

She gives me an odd look, but I mean it. I want her to stay here on the mountain with me. I've never felt like this about a woman before, never.

She looks out at the sunrise, her hair shimmering golden in the light. If I could capture this moment and bottle it up forever then I would.

It doesn't take long to pack up our camp, and then we're ready to head down the mountain. The path back is all downhill and can be done in one day's hike.

She puts her hand in mine, and I clasp it tight, holding onto her as we set off down the path.

We talk on the way back, getting to know each other. She finally comes clean, telling me about how she lied to get the assignment.

She's nervous telling me, but I laugh at the boldness of it. She obviously wants this so much, to be a journalist. I love that she pushed herself out of her comfort zone to get what she wanted.

"The thing is," she says. "Now that I've spent time in the outdoors, I love it."

She's beaming and I feel a surge of pride, that I showed her the mountain and she fell in love with it, but did she fall in love with me? Because I know in my heart, that I love this woman. That I want her in my life.

Brooklyn talks about the article she's going to write, and I'm caught up in her excitement. But then it hits me.

She did everything she could to get this opportunity because she wants so badly to be a journalist. Brooklyn's got ambitions, and with her bold attitude I'm sure she'll make her dream happen. There's no way she'll want to give it all up to come and live in a tiny town halfway up the mountain.

I couldn't ask her to do that, as much as I want to.

She squeezes my hand. "What's wrong?"

Her look is so innocent, so happy, that I don't want to ruin the moment.

I plaster a smile on my face. "Nothing at all."

It's a few hours later that we reach the start of the track and my pick-up truck. I throw our gear in the back and drive to her hotel.

As we're driving, she turns her phone on to see if there's signal. It immediately rings.

"Hello?"

Her face falls as she talks. I can only hear one side of the conversation but it doesn't sound good. We reach the hotel and I pull over just as she hangs up.

"That was Lilia." She already told me all about her best friend. "Kelvin found out I lied."

It takes me a moment to remember that Kelvin is the editor of the magazine she's writing the article for.

"How did he find out?"

"Did some digging on me. I guess you should never lie to a journalist."

"Are you in trouble."

"Big time. He's furious. He wants my back in the office pronto."

My heart sinks, I know where this is going. I thought we would have more time together, that I could convince her to stay a few more nights with me. But she must go.

"Will you still have your internship?"

She shrugs. "I don't know."

She looks so worried that I don't want to add to her concerns by telling her my feelings. I don't know if she feels the same. And she's too concerned about her situation right now.

"I need to go, Chase."

She bites her lower lip and I see the anxiety she's feeling. I put my hands on her shoulders to calm her down.

She looks up at me, her eyes finding mine.

"Go, Brooklyn, write your article and show him how good you are."

A tiny smile breaks through the worry on her face."

"Thank you."

I put on a smile I don't feel as I wave her off. As her old car swerves down the road, it feels like a piece of me is driving away with her.

BROOKLYN

Two weeks later…

My eyes scan the last lines of the article and then underneath, the byline.

By Brooklyn Jones.

My name in print for the very first time. I should be happy; I should be celebrating. But I'm sitting alone at a cafe opposite the office, feeling nothing but emptiness.

It's been two weeks since I came down from the mountain, as Lilia likes to dramatically call it. She reckons I came back a changed woman, and she's not wrong.

It wasn't just the time in the outdoors that changed me, it was my time with Chase.

My mind goes back to the night we spent under the stars. Just thinking about his hands on me makes my core ache with longing. We shared a connection, something powerful and overwhelming. The kind of connection that you don't realize you've got until it's gone.

When I left him on the mountain, I was so worried about losing my internship, that I never told him how much our time together meant to me. It wasn't until I got back to Seattle that I realized how much I missed him. His touch, his smile, his easy conversation.

I could have emailed the tourist office; it wouldn't have taken much to find his phone number. But did he want to be found? Was I just some city girl that he slept with one night under the stars? Maybe he does that on all his guided trail hikes and I naively thought it was special.

So, I didn't call, and he didn't track me down either.

I sigh. At least I'll always have the memory of that night together, I don't regret a thing.

My gazes goes back to the article in front of me. I read my name again trying to conjure up the excitement, I know I should feel.

Kelvin was angry that I'd lied to him about my outdoor experience, but he was also impressed by my boldness. He gave me a dressing down and told me that article better be on his desk in the morning. I stayed up all night to write it and emailed it to him, waiting anxiously for his reply.

And he loved it. There were revisions needed, and I

worked with him on them. But when I sent the final copy, he even smiled and told me I'd done a good job.

It should be a happy day, seeing my name in print, but here I am, alone in a coffee shop and I feel anything but happy.

I lower the magazine and my heart skips a beat. Standing outside, looking in at me, is Chase.

My mouth drops open as I drink him in. His shaggy hair is pulled back into a man bun, and his beard has been trimmed. His khakis have been replaced with jeans and his walking boots with sneakers.

He pulls at his polo neck shirt, looking out of place on Maddison Street with the skyscrapers behind him instead of a mountain.

"Chase?"

He strides into the coffee shop and I stand up to meet him. My heart beats wildly, hopefully.

"What are you doing here?"

"I came to see you."

He catches my hand in his. My pulse jumps under my skin and I can barely breath.

"Why?"

"Because I can't be without you, Brooklyn."

My heart melts. It's everything I've been needing to hear. I open my mouth to speak, and he holds up a hand to silence me.

"I know the city is your home and you've got a good thing going on here. I can't ask you to give that up." He takes a big breath. "I've been doing a lot of thinking, and I'll move here. I'll move to Seattle so I can be with you."

His look is so sincere, so earnest. He's saying everything I want to hear, but it's not right. Chase's whole life is on that mountain. He works there, he grew up there, he belongs there.

"I can't let you do that."

He shakes his head. "I've thought it all out. I'll get a job in one of the big parks, we can make a life here. I don't care what I do as long as I'm with you."

He clasps both my hands together and his look is so intense so full of meaning. "If you'll have me."

It's everything I want to hear and my heart yearns for him, but I can't let him sacrifice this much for me. He's a man of the mountain, he'd only be unhappy here. He already looks uncomfortable in his city clothes. I can't do that to him.

"You belong on the mountain."

"I belong with you."

His lips meet mine, and the last two weeks of loneliness and hurt come out in that kiss. I need to be with him, but not like this. I pull away.

"Chase, I can't let you do that. There's another way." I bite my lip because while he was planning to move to the city, I made some plans of my own. "You don't have to move here. I'll move to you."

He shakes his head. "No, I can't let you give up your dream here."

"I don't have to. Kelvin's offered me freelance journalist work. I don't have to be based here. I can work from anywhere as long as I go do my assignments every month. It'll mean a few days a month away for work, but other than that, I can base myself wherever I want."

A smile spreads over his face as he begins to understand. "You want to move to Maple Falls?"

"I fell in love with the mountain just as much as I fell in love with you."

He lifts me into his arms and right up off the ground making me squeal.

"Let's go get your things, honey, because I'm taking you home."

Five years later…

There's a rustling in the tent and I feel a small body climbing over me.

"Mommy, I heard something."

Finn's anxious face appears next to mine in the darkness. I reach an arm out and pull my son down to the floor next to me.

"It was probably the wind, sweetie."

"I think it was a bear."

Tucking him into the sleeping bag, I plant a kiss on his forehead.

"You stay right there between me and Daddy, we'll keep you safe."

He snuggles in between us, and I adjust my pregnant belly so it's away from his squirming body. Chase rolls over and puts a protective arm around his son.

"There's no bears this far down the mountain. I wouldn't let you or mommy camp where a bear could get you."

A gust of wind rustles the tent, and Finn pulls the covers over his head, hiding.

"It's okay, buddy, just the wind." Chase grins in the darkness. "Now give your mommy and the baby some space and come lie this side of me."

Finn clambers over Chase and settles in on the other side of him.

"You okay?" he mouths to me, his face full of concern.

He didn't want to come camping in my third trimester, but I insisted. I wanted to feel the fresh mountain air one more time before I get too close to my due date to risk a mountain hike.

We're up near the lakes where we spent our first night under the stars together. We've taken Finn out hiking since he was a baby, first strapped to my front and then, as he got older, in a toddler backpack on Chase's back.

Chase has shown me every trail and every camping spot. Both Finn and the baby growing in my belly were conceived on the side of Maple Mountain.

My dream of being a journalist has been realized. I write freelance for outdoors and parenting magazines.

Chase and Finn come on most of my assignments. They're like family holidays, where I get paid to hike the trails of the northwest.

Finn's breathing deepens and I know he's gone back to sleep. Now he's asleep again I can relax. My arms wrap around Chase's body, not able to get too close with my big belly in the way.

Soon, he's snoring gently, and I lie quietly, listening to the sounds of them sleeping and the wind in the trees, thinking how blessed I am to have my family and to have the mountain. How glad I am I took a chance and discovered my two great loves.

MEN OF MAPLE MOUNTAIN

Complete the Men of Maple Mountain series for your swoon worthy OTT alphas.

Each book is a standalone but best enjoyed in together.

Men of Maple Mountain

Mountain Man's Obsession – Colette & Bear

Mountain Man's Captive – Annie & Colton

Mountain Man's Virgin – Brooklyn & Chase

Mountain Man's Muse – Heather & Kane

Mountain Man's Redemption – Bethany & Ewan

Mountain Man's First Time – Ursula & Kit

Companion titles

Mountain Man's Healer - Jenny & Rowan

All the Scars we Cannot See - Emily & Sam

Boxset Collection

Men of Maple Mountain Books 1-7

Includes a bonus short story:

Mountain Man's Steamy Anniversary - (Bear & Colette)

How far would you go to protect the one you love?

Ava

It's the last stop on my latest book tour: the sleepy town of Sycamore Mountain.

Every stop has been the same, with fans asking me when the next book is coming out and if my lead character will ever find love.

But how do you write about love when you've never experienced it?

Then I meet Holden, the burly mountain man who's providing security.

When we get stuck in his cabin, Holden keeps me safe, calming my fears about a deranged fan.

Holden doesn't talk much, but he loves dirty books,

and when he reads them out loud to me, I melt right off the page.

Holden

I've been obsessed with Ava Greyson ever since I discovered her books with the strong, wild heroines. When she comes to the Sycamore Mountain Annual Book Festival, I'm first in line to volunteer.

When an obsessed fan goes too far, I get the chance to be her hero.

I take Ava up the mountain to keep her safe. But once I've got her in my cabin, I'll do whatever it takes to keep her there.

She must never find out what I've done to protect her...

His Big Book Stack is a shy girl and mountain man, forced proximity steamy romance. Featuring an over protective and obsessed alpha male and an innocent curvy girl.

Keep reading for an exclusive excerpt or visit:
mybook.to/HisBigBookStack

HIS BIG BOOK STACK

CHAPTER ONE

A bead of sweat trickles down my back, and I stand up, hoping the audience doesn't hear the squelching noise my sweaty thighs make as they leave the leather seat.

It's got to be close to one hundred degrees outside, and even with the air conditioning whirring away in here, it's hot, especially under the lights that have been set up for the makeshift stage in the town hall.

"That brings us to the question and answer section of the talk."

Hands shoot into the air, and I squint into the audience, shielding my eyes from the spotlight. A woman in a tight red top waves her arm earnestly, and I nod in her direction.

One of the stagehands trots over with the microphone and hands it to the woman.

"Hi," she gasps. "I'm a big fan."

The smile that spreads across my face is genuine. I

love doing book festivals. Meeting my readers is just the best.

"Thank you."

"So, I love that Kim is this tough female detective…"

I know even before she says it what's coming next. My stomach sinks, but I keep the smile plastered on my face.

"But her co-workers have all partnered up. Will Kim ever find love?"

I stifle a groan. It's the same question I've been asked at every single festival up and down the country. "When will Kim fall in love?" As if being a bad-ass detective solving heinous crimes and catching baddies isn't enough.

You've got to give the readers what they want. At least that's what my agent told me.

And I'm trying, I really am.

I wrote a side plot spanning three books for Kim's sidekick to get romantically attached. It was stilted and awkward, and it was just a side plot. I could fudge over the details.

But Kim is the main character, the heroine of a ten-book series. If she's going to fall in love, it needs to be a big deal. It needs to be with a kick-ass alpha man who deserves her, and it has to be a big, big love.

But how do you write about love if you've never experienced it?

The woman is looking at me anxiously, waiting for my answer.

I tilt my head in what I hope is a mysterious way. "Let's say, I'm working on something for Kim."

I nod to a man with his hand up, but the woman keeps hold of the mic.

"What does that mean, exactly? Will Kim find someone special, someone to combat her loneliness?"

Damn this character I've created. I made Kim's loneliness a thing so there would be empathy for the hard-nosed detective. She hunts killers by day, the hero of her town, but comes home to an empty house at night.

But my fans don't want Kim to be lonely anymore. There's mounting pressure on social media, and someone started an online group called Get Kim Hitched.

Which is why I agreed with my agent—sorry, why I was bullied by my agent into writing a love story into the next book.

The deal was it would be the final book in the series. I'm tired of Kim, tired of writing crime. I'm ready to retire the series.

But it's hard to retire a series that my readers love so much.

"Yes," I say. "Kim will get her happy ending."

The woman beams, and there are excited murmurs from the audience.

My gut clenches. I've said it out loud now.

Up to this point I'd been evasive, but now I've said it. Someone will be tweeting it, and the whole internet will know by morning, so now I'll have to stick to it.

I swallow hard and take a sip of water.

A kernel of doubt flickers in my gut. I hope I can deliver what my readers want. I hope my attempt at writing a love story is close enough to the real thing to make people believe it.

I nod at a woman in the back row, and she stands up and waits for the mic to reach her.

She's staring at me intently. My skin prickles under her gaze.

A chill runs down my back. I shouldn't have chosen her. I couldn't see her properly in the back row, but I don't like to leave anyone out.

Finally, the mic reaches the woman, and she snatches it out of the stagehand's grasp.

"What can you tell me about the death threats?"

A ripple of surprise goes round the room. I swallow hard, and my eyes dart to the wings where my publicist is looking just as shocked as I am.

No one's meant to know about the death threats. Sure, there's the nasty online trolling that unfortunately any woman in the public eye gets. But recently it's taken a more sinister turn.

I've received a series of emails, each time from a different dummy address, each one explaining explicitly what they'll do to me as if I'm one of the victims in my books.

The police are tracking the culprit, and someone must have leaked information.

"I have no comment on that."

"But it is true that you've had death threats?"

I shield my eyes to squint at the woman. She looks smug, a reporter looking for a reaction and a story. I won't give her one.

"You can speak to my publicist if you have any further questions, but this session is for my readers, not the press."

I take a sip of water, using the time to steady my nerves while the stagehand wrestles the microphone back.

I take a deep breath, then point to a man with his hand in the air.

"What's your writing process?"

I'm back on familiar territory, and as I answer the man's question, my breathing comes back under control.

It's not until I've taken several more questions that I become aware of a man standing in the shadows.

He's clad all in black, almost blending in with the stage curtains. His face is hooded by the heavy drapes at the side of the hall. But I can tell he's watching me. I can feel his eyes on me.

My body tenses. I falter halfway through my sentence.

My breathing gets shallow, and the room suddenly feels closed in.

"Ava?"

Someone says my name, but it sounds far away. All I can focus on is the man in black—the man who's come to kill me.

The room starts to spin, and the man rushes forward. He's got a gun, no, a knife, no… My eyes go wide as I see his hands. Large, rough, empty hands.

The last thing I remember is those big, rough hands catching me before I drop to the floor in a dead faint.

To keep reading visit:
mybook.to/HisBigBookStack

BOOKS BY SADIE KING

Maple Springs

Men of Maple Mountain

All the Single Dads

Candy's Café

Small Town Sisters

Fudge and the Firefighter (Christmas)

What the Fudge (Christmas)

Sunset Coast

Sunset Security

Men of the Sea

Underground Crows MC

Kings County

Kings of Fire

King's Cops

For a full list of titles visit the Sadie King website

www.authorsadieking.com

ABOUT THE AUTHOR

Sadie King is a USA Today Best Selling Author of short instalove romance.

She lives in New Zealand with her ex-military husband and raucous young son.

When she's not writing she loves catching waves with her son, running along the beach, and good wine, preferably drunk with a book in hand.

Keep in touch when you sign up for her newsletter. You'll even snag yourself a free short romance!

www.authorsadieking.com/free

www.ingramcontent.com/pod-product-compliance
Lightning Source LLC
Chambersburg PA
CBHW021808150726
47989CB00004B/1831